Curious Tom Gobbler

ANNE STRILCHUK

Illustrated by David Matley

Tellwell Talent
www.tellwell.ca

ISBN
978-0-2288-4461-7 (Paperback)

Acknowledgements

A huge thanks to my cousin David Matley for his wonderful illustrations. David would like to thank his wife Diane Orchard-Matley for her help in photographing his drawings.

And thank you to Ruth Roedler for proofreading and to her grandchildren Blake and Emily Roedler for critiquing my story.

Dedication

I dedicate this book to everyone who is curious about this wonderful world we live in, and to my children, Jennifer (Rudy), and Steven (Paula), and my awesome grandchildren Nicole, Jake and Kurt Schulz, and Cameron and Daniel Strilchuk and my granddogs Chloe and Piper.

A few years ago, on the Diamond Turkey Farm east of the little town of Carstairs, an interesting event occurred. A baby turkey was born. No, that wasn't the interesting event, it was because he was different from any other turkey.

Instead of saying, "Peep, peep, peep," he asked, "Why? Why? Why?" He was always asking his mom and dad, his sisters and brothers, his cousins and aunts and uncles about everything. "Why do you say gobble, gobble, gobble? Why do we all look the same? Why do we eat worms? Where do they come from? Why is the grass green?"

His proper name was Thomas Aquinas Gobbler but because he was always asking questions, his family and relatives and friends started calling him Curious Tom or CT for short. "Mom," he asked, "Why did the chicken cross the road?" "Dad," he queried, "Why does a spider spin a web in a circle?"

One day, after listening to his many questions, CT's mother sighed, "You are such a recalcitrant little turkey!" CT liked the word and asked, "What does re-cal-ci-trant mean?" She replied, "It means you are stubborn. You should learn to enjoy our happy life here instead of asking so many questions!"

But soon his friends became bored with all his questions. They couldn't understand why he needed to know about everything when their only question was, "What time is dinner?" So, they started ignoring him or making fun of him or avoiding him. He became very sad. Even his own family ignored him because they couldn't answer his questions.

CT is very sad because his family and others make fun of him, ignore him and won't answer his questions.

One day, as he sat by himself in the corner of a field, he had an idea. He asked himself why he was staying on this farm if no one could help him, so he decided to leave the farm. As he left the field, he noticed his friend Chloe the sheep who asked where he was going. He said, "I'm thinking of leaving the farm. I want to find the answers to all of my questions." Chloe said, "Don't do that CT, it's a dark and crazy world out there!" CT replied that it was his destiny and he said goodbye to Chloe.

He packed a little bag full of corn and seeds and headed west. He met a very friendly raccoon walking along the road and asked him who he was and where he was going. The raccoon replied, "I'm Ronnie and I am on my way to the woods near here to meet my family." So, they travelled together for a while and then Ronnie said goodbye.

CT decides to leave the farm and heads west looking for answers to his many questions.

He was a little bit afraid of the big machines that whizzed past him. He often hid in the ditch until they left. He was curious about where they were going and why. So he followed them.

CT is afraid when big vehicles whiz by him so he hides in a ditch. DM 2020

Soon CT came to the little town of Carstairs. He wondered why there were so many buildings and so many people.

1909 EST.

ANTIQUES

BOOKS

TOWN OF
CARSTAIRS
POPULATION 4,729 APPROX.

CT discovers
the town of
Carstairs.

DM 2020

He came to a yard where he spotted a little girl swinging slowly back and forth on a swing. Her name was Annabelle. She looked very sad. CT wondered why she was sad. He slowly stepped towards her and looked up at her face.

y chance, CT comes to a yard where there is a
ry sad and quiet little girl on a swing, her name is Annabelle. DM2020

She looked down at him and at first was a bit afraid. But then she became curious about where he had come from. She reached out and started stroking his feathers very gently. This felt incredibly wonderful to CT. He took out his little bag and offered her some corn. She laughed and said, "Thank you very much but I just ate."

Annabelle gently strokes CT's soft feathers.

She then asked who he was and where he was from. CT introduced himself and lifted his wing and pointed to the east as he told her about the farm. She told him her name was Annabelle.

They spent the rest of the day together, walking through the town, visiting the Carstairs Heritage Centre and all the other interesting places in town.

They visited the town and the Carstairs Heritage Centre and CT got answers to some of his questions.

On their way back, Annabelle and CT met a chipmunk who was busily working under an oak tree. His name was Chippy. CT asked him, "Why are you collecting acorns?" Chippy replied, "I store them and during the winter they make a nice snack." CT found that answer to be very interesting.

When they returned to her house, she took CT inside to meet her mother. "Mom, may I keep CT?" she asked. Well, as you can imagine, her mother was taken aback but then she thought about it. First of all, her daughter wasn't sneezing. She was usually allergic to almost everything. Secondly, her daughter seldom talked but here she was chatting away. Thirdly, she had never seen her daughter so happy, so she answered, "Yes Annabelle if nobody claims him."

Thankfully, no one claimed him so CT stayed with Annabelle and her parents for a very long time. He found the answers to so many of his questions and she had finally found a friend.

THE END

Annabelle does keep CT and they become best friends for a very long time.

Turkey Terms

Caruncle – brightly coloured growths on the throat region. Turns bright red when the turkey is upset or during courtship.

Gizzard – a part of a bird's stomach that contains tiny stones. It helps them grind up food for digestion.

Hen – a female turkey.

Poult – a baby turkey. A chick.

Snood – the flap of skin that hangs over the turkey's beak. Turns bright red when the turkey is upset or during courtship.

Tom – a male turkey. Also known as a gobbler.

Wattle – the flap of skin under the turkey's chin. Turns bright red when the turkey is upset or during courtship.

Scientific genus and species: Meleagris gallopavo.

snood

caruncle

wattle

Author: Anne Strilchuk was born in Ottawa, Ontario, Canada. In 1967, Centennial year, she became a stewardess for Air Canada, was based in Calgary, Alberta, and was married. She has two children, five grandchildren and two granddogs. She moved to Carstairs, Alberta in 1982, became a teacher aide, librarian and councillor but is now retired. She enjoys reading, writing, painting, music, gardening, family and friends, coffee and cookies.

Illustrator: David Matley lives in Ottawa, Ontario, Canada, with his wife Diane. They have a son, Tim, and a daughter, Chris. He enjoys drawing cartoons, playing golf and slo-pitch, and watching history shows. He has a B.A. in history and worked in publishing at the National Archives of Canada for many years.

CPSIA information can be obtained
at www.ICGtesting.com
Printed in the USA
BVHW091843111220
595318BV00001B/1